It's A Jungle Out There

Ed Miliano

To Anne, Aoife and Oisín
—EM

First published 1997 by
WOLFHOUND PRESS Ltd
68 Mountjoy Square
Dublin 1

©1997 Ed Miliano

Wolfhound Press receives financial assistance from the Arts Council/An Chomhairle Ealaíon, Dublin.

British Library Cataloguing in Publication Data

A catalogue record for this book is available from the British Library.

ISBN 0-86327-570-2

Design and typesetting: Ed Miliano
Colour separations: Graphic Reproductions
Printed and bound in Belgium by Proost N.V.

It's a jungle out there.

Danger lurks
everywhere.

Up high in the sky.

Down low on the ground.

Creatures so small and so large,

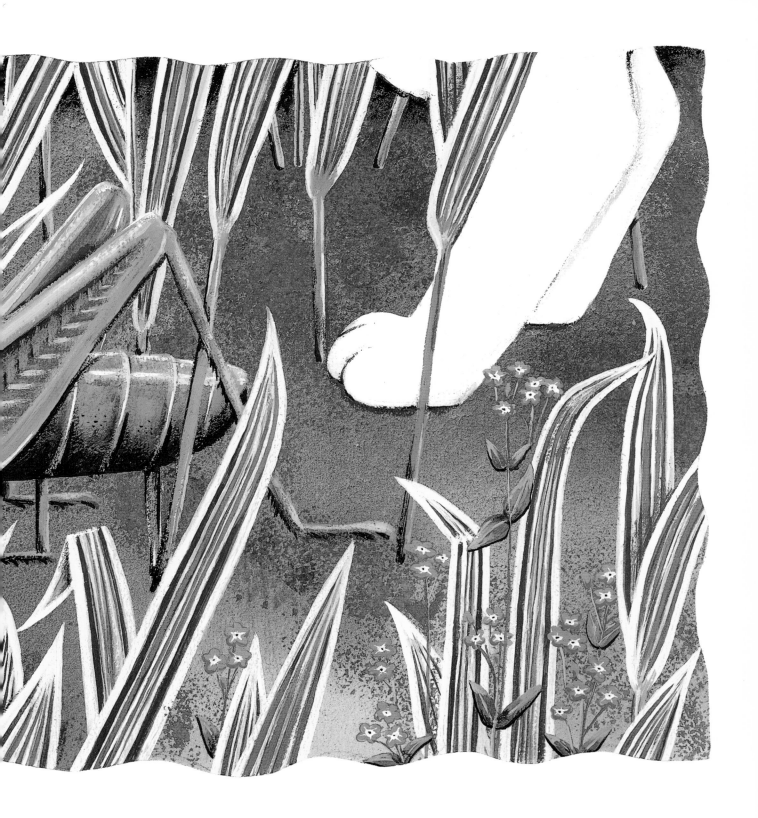

someone has to take charge.

I am that someone.

I am that cat.

Wild and white with eagle eyesight.

Sleek and fast, no one gets past!

All day long,
I watch and I wait.

See the beetles stalk…
Like giants they walk.

Quietly I spy

these shadows that fly.

The ants, they are marching,

creeping and crawling.

Spiders weave webs to trap me.

Buzz, buzz, buzz
is all I hear.

Bees are buzzing
everywhere.

Twice a day I walk the walls of the jungle,

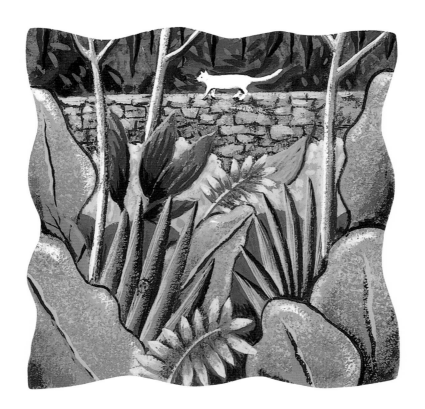

keeping outsiders out, and insiders in.

By the end of the day
I am tired
and I am hungry
and I long for my bed.

I have a bite to eat and lie down to sleep.
And I say to myself…

It's a jungle out there.